IF YOU GIVE A
MOOSE A MUFFIN

by Laura Joffe Numeroff

illustrated by Felicia Bond

A Laura Geringer Book

An Imprint of HarperCollins*Publishers*

If You Give a Moose a Muffin
Text copyright © 1991 by Laura Numeroff
Illustrations copyright © 1991 by Felicia Bond
Manufactured in China. All rights reserved.

Library of Congress Cataloging-in-Publication Data

Numeroff, Laura Joffe.
  If you give a moose a muffin / by Laura Joffe Numeroff ;
illustrated by Felicia Bond.
    p.   cm.
  "A Laura Geringer book."
  Summary: Chaos can ensue if you give a moose a muffin and start
him on a cycle of urgent requests.
ISBN-10: 0-06-134954-2 — ISBN-13: 978-0-06-134954-6
  [1. Moose—Fiction.]   I. Bond, Felicia, ill.   II. Title.
PZ7.N9641d   1991   91-2207
[E]—dc20   CIP
                                                                 AC

is a registered trademark of HarperCollins Publishers

For Alice and Emily, the two best sisters
anyone could ever possibly want!
L.J.N.

For Antoine, Nahem, Jennifer, Santos, Brian and Crystal
F.B.

If you give a moose a muffin,

he'll want some jam to go with it.

So you'll bring out some of your mother's homemade blackberry jam.

When he's finished eating the muffin, he'll want another.

And another.

And another.
When they're all gone,
he'll ask you to make more.

You'll have to go to the store to get some muffin mix.

He'll want to go with you.

When he opens the door and feels how chilly it is, he'll ask to borrow a sweater.

When he puts the sweater on, he'll notice one of the buttons is loose.

He'll ask for a needle and thread.

He'll start sewing.
The button will remind him of the
puppets his grandmother
used to make.

So he'll ask for some old socks.

He'll make sock puppets.

When they're done, he'll want to
put on a puppet show.

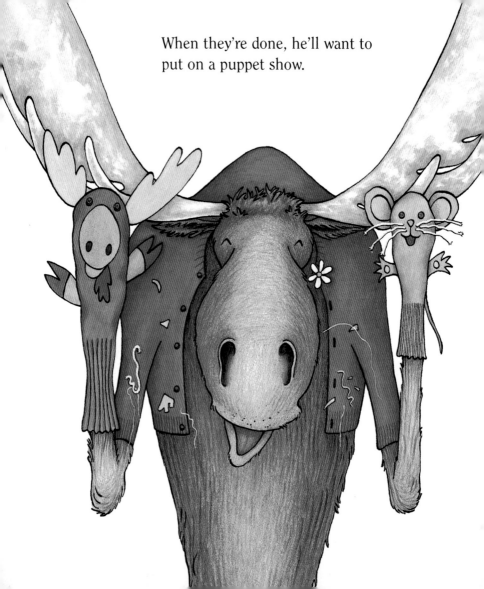

He'll need some cardboard
and paints.

Then he'll ask you to help make the scenery.

When the scenery is finished, he'll get behind the couch. But his antlers will stick out.

So he'll ask for something to cover them up.

You'll bring him a sheet from your bed.

When he sees the sheet, he'll remember
he wants to be a ghost for Halloween.

He'll try it on and shout,

"BOO!"

It'll scare him
so much, he'll knock
over the paints.

So he'll use the sheet
to clean up the mess.

Then he'll ask for some soap to wash it out.

He'll probably want to hang the sheet up to dry.

He'll go outside to put it on the clothesline.

When he's out in the yard, he'll see
your mother's blackberry bushes.

Seeing the blackberries
will remind him of
her jam.

He'll probably ask you for some.

And chances are . . .

if you give him the jam,

he'll want a muffin to go with it.